DO LIKE KYLA

DO LIKE KYLA

by Angela Johnson
paintings by James E. Ransome

Orchard Books / An Imprint of Scholastic Inc.

New York Toronto London Auckland Sydney
Mexico City New Delhi Hong Kong Buenos Aires

ISBN 0-531-07040-9

21 20 19 18   12 13 14 15/0

Printed in the United States of America   08

Book design by Mina Greenstein.
The text of this book is set in 18-point ITC Esprit Medium.
The illustrations are oil paintings, reproduced in halftone.

To my brothers, Keith and Kent

A.J.

To the two most important women in my life,
the late Mrs. Ruby G. Ransome and Lesa M. Cline

J.E.R.

In the morning my big sister Kyla stands at the window, tapping at the birds.
I do like Kyla, only standing on the bed.

Kyla pulls her sweater over her head and stretches.
I do like Kyla.

We sit in front of the big mirror in our room, and Kyla braids her hair with quick fingers.

I try to do like Kyla in front of the mirror.
Kyla says, "Beautiful!"
I do like Kyla and say, "Beautiful!"

Oatmeal and apples for breakfast, and I do like Kyla, pouring honey on everything.

Mama says, "Lots of sunshine today."

Kyla kisses the sunbeam on the dog's head.
I do like Kyla.

We're going to the store so Kyla helps me put my coat on.
"Warm now," she says.
I do like Kyla and say, "Warm now."

Got me some purple snow boots like Kyla, and we both crunch, crunch in the snow all the way to the store.

Past the big store window, I see myself.
I do like Kyla and skip past the window, watching....

In the good-smelling store Kyla asks for cheese,
a bag of apples, and a jar of jam.

The man in the white apron says, "Goodbye and be good."
I do like Kyla and say, "OK, I will."

Kyla says, "Want to follow our footsteps back home?"
I do, just like Kyla.

Step, step, step.

"Read me a book, Kyla."
Kyla reads to me under the kitchen table.
I do like her and say, "The end," after the last page.

It's almost nighttime at the window.
Kyla says, "Birds must be asleep."

I tap at the window...

and Kyla does just like me.